# BREATH OF ALLAH

BY

## SAX ROHMER

**British Library Cataloguing-in-Publication Data**
A catalogue record for this book is available from the
British Library

# CONTENTS

# SAX ROHMER

Sax Rohmer was born in Ladywood, Birmingham, England in 1883. Hailing from a working class family, Rohmer briefly pursued careers in civil service and the theatre before turning to writing. In 1903, his first published work, 'The Mysterious Mummy', appeared in *Pearson's Weekly*. Rohmer continued to write weird fiction, and his major breakthrough came in 1912, when the first Fu-Manchu novel, *The Mystery of Dr. Fu-Manchu*, was serialized over a period of eight months. Rohmer's story of Fu-Manchu – an evil genius described as "the yellow peil incarnate in one man" – played off the imagined threat of Asian immigrants which was common in that day, and was an instant bestseller. Fu-Manchu went on to star in thirteen more novels, and – combined with his more conventional detective fiction – made Rohmer one of the most successful and well-paid authors of his day. Rohmer was a prolific writer right up to his death, which came as a result of an outbreak of Asian Flu.

# BREATH OF ALLAH

## I

For close upon a week I had been haunting the purlieus of the Mûski, attired as a respectable dragoman, my face and hands reduced to a deeper shade of brown by means of a water-colour paint (I had to use something that could be washed off and greasepaint is useless for purposes of actual disguise) and a neat black moustache, fixed to my lip with spirit-gum. In his story 'Beyond the Pale', Rudyard Kipling has trounced the man who enquires too deeply into native life; but if everybody thought with Kipling we should never have had a Lane or a Burton and I should have continued in unbroken scepticism regarding the reality of magic. Whereas, because of the matters which I am about to set forth, for ten minutes of my life I found myself a trembling slave of the unknown.

Let me explain at once that my undignified masquerade was not prompted by mere curiosity or the quest of the pomegranate, it was undertaken as the natural sequel to a letter received from Messrs Moses, Murphy and Co., the firm which I represented in Egypt, containing curious matters affording much food for reflection. 'We would ask you,' ran the communication, 'to renew your enquiries into the particular composition of the perfume "Breath of Allah", of which you obtained us a sample at a cost which we regarded as excessive. It appears to consist in the blending of certain obscure essential oils and gum-resins; and the nature of some of these has defied analysis to date. Over a hundred experiments have been made to discover substitutes for the missing essences, but without success; and as we are now in a position to arrange for the manufacture of Oriental perfume on an extensive scale, we should be prepared to make it *well worth your while* (the last four words characteristically underlined in red ink) if you could obtain for us a correct copy of the original prescription.'

The letter went on to say that it was proposed to establish a separate company for the exploitation of the new perfume, with a registered address in Cairo and a 'manufactory' in some suitably inaccessible spot in the Near East.

I pondered deeply over these matters. The scheme was a good one and could not fail to reap considerable profits; for, given extensive advertising, there is always a large and monied public for a new smell. The particular blend of liquid fragrance to which the letter referred was assured of a good sale at a high price, not alone in Egypt, but throughout the capitals of the world, provided it could be put upon the market; but the proposition of manufacture was beset with extraordinary difficulties.

The tiny vial which I had despatched to Birmingham nearly twelve months before had cost me close upon £100 to procure, for the reason that 'Breath of Allah' was the secret property of an old and aristocratic Egyptian family whose great wealth and exclusiveness rendered them unapproachable. By dint of diligent enquiry I had discovered the *attár* to whom was entrusted certain final processes in the preparation of the perfume – only to learn that he was ignorant of its exact composition. But although he had assured me (and I did not doubt his word) that not one grain had hitherto passed out of the possession of the family, I had succeeded in procuring a small quantity of the precious fluid.

Messrs Moses, Murphy and Co. had made all the necessary arrangements for placing it upon the market, only to learn, as this eventful letter advised me, that the most skilled chemists whose services were obtainable had failed to analyse it.

One morning, then, in my assumed character, I was proceeding along the Sharia el-Hamzâwi seeking for some scheme whereby I might win the confidence of Mohammed er-Rahmân the *attár*, or perfumer. I had quitted the house in the Darb el-Ahmar which was my base of operations but a few minutes earlier, and as I approached the corner of the street a voice called from a window directly above my head:

'Saïd! Saïd!'

Without supposing that the call referred to myself, I glanced up, and met the gaze of an old Egyptian of respectable appearance who was regarding me from above. Shading his eyes with a gnarled hand – 'Surely,' he cried, 'it is none other than Saïd the nephew of Yûssuf Khalig! *Es-selâm'aleykûm, Saïd!*'

*'Aleykûm, es-selâm,'* I replied, and stood there looking up at him.

'Would you perform a little service for me, Saïd?' he continued. 'It will occupy you but an hour and you may earn five piastres.'

'Willingly,' I replied, not knowing to what the mistake of this evidently half-blind old man might lead me.

I entered the door and mounted the stairs to the room in which he was, to find that he lay upon a scantily covered *dïwan* by the open window.

'Praise be to Allah (whose name be exalted)!' he exclaimed, 'that I am thus fortunately enabled to fulfil my obligations. I sometimes suffer from an old serpent bite, my son, and this morning it has obliged me to abstain from all movement. I am called Abdûl the Porter, of whom you will have heard your uncle speak: and although I have long retired from active labour, myself, I contract for the supply of porters and carriers of all descriptions and for all purposes; conveying fair ladies to the *hammâm*, youth to the bridal, and death to

6

the grave. Now, it was written that you should arrive at this timely hour.'

I considered it highly probable that it was also written how I should shortly depart if this garrulous old man continued to inflict upon me details of his absurd career. However –

'I have a contract with the merchant, Mohammed er-Rahmân of the Sûk el-Attârin,' he continued, 'which it has always been my custom personally to carry out.'

The words almost caused me to catch my breath; and my opinion of Abdul the Porter changed extraordinarily. Truly my lucky star had guided my footsteps that morning!

'Do not misunderstand me,' he added. 'I refer not to the transport of his wares to Suez, to Zagazig, to Mecca, to Aleppo, to Baghdad, Damascus, Kandahar, and Pekin; although the whole of these vast enterprises is entrusted to none other than the only son of my father: I speak, now, of the bearing of a small though heavy box from the great magazine and manufactory of Mohammed er-Rahmân at Shubra, to his shop in the Sûk el-Attârin, a matter which I have arranged for him on the eve of the Molid en-Nebi (birthday of the Prophet) for the past five-and-thirty years. Every one of my porters to whom I might entrust this special charge is otherwise employed; hence my observation that it was written how none other than yourself should pass beneath this window at a certain fortunate hour.'

Fortunate indeed had that hour been for me, and my pulse beat far from normally as I put the question:

'Why, O Father Abdul, do you attach so much importance to this seemingly trivial matter?'

The face of Abdul the Porter, which resembled that of an intelligent mule, assumed an expression of low cunning.

'The question is well conceived,' he said, raising a long forefinger and wagging it at me. 'And who in all Cairo knows so much of the secrets of the great as Abdul the Know-all, Abdul the Taciturn! Ask me of the fabled wealth of Karafa Bey and I will name you every one of his possessions and entertain you with a calculation of his income, which I have worked out in *nûss-faddah*! Ask me of the amber mole upon the shoulder of the Princess Azîza and I will describe it to you in such a manner as to ravish your soul! Whisper, my son' – he bent towards me confidentially – 'once a year the merchant Mohammed er-Rahmân prepares for the Lady Zuleyka a quantity of the perfume which impious tradition has called "Breath of Allah". The father of Mohammed er-Rahmân prepared it for the mother of the Lady Zuleyka and his father before him for the lady of that day who held the secret – the secret which has belonged to the women of this family since the reign of the Khalîf el-Hakîm from whose favourite wife they are descended. To her, the wife of the Khalîf, the first *dirhem* [drachm] ever distilled of the perfume

8

was presented in a gold vase, together with the manner of its preparation, by the great wizard and physician Ibn Sina of Bokhara [Avicenna].'

'You are well called Abdul the Know-all!' I cried in admiration. 'Then the secret is held by Mohammed er-Rahmân?'

'Not so, my son,' replied Abdul. 'Certain of the essences employed are brought, in sealed vessels, from the house of the Lady Zuleyka, as is also the brass coffer containing the writing of Ibn Sina; and throughout the measuring of the quantities, the secret writing never leaves her hand.'

'What, the Lady Zuleyka attends in person?'

Abdul the Porter inclined his head serenely.

'On the eve of the birthday of the Prophet, the Lady Zuleyka visits the shop of Mohammed er-Rahmân, accompanied by an *imâm* from one of the great mosques.'

'Why by an *imâm*, Father Abdul?'

'There is a magical ritual which must be observed in the distillation of the perfume, and each essence is blessed in the name of one of the four archangels; and the whole operation must commence at the hour of midnight on the eve of the Molid en-Nebi.'

He peered at me triumphantly.

'Surely,' I protested, 'an experienced *attâr* such as Mohammed er-Rahmân would readily recognise these secret ingredients by their smell?'

'A great pan of burning charcoal,' whispered Abdul dramatically, 'is placed upon the floor of the room, and throughout the operation the attendant *imám* casts pungent spices upon it, whereby the nature of the secret essences is rendered unrecognisable. It is time you depart, my son, to the shop of Mohammed, and I will give you a writing making you known to him. Your task will be to carry the materials necessary for the secret operation (which takes place tonight) from the magazine of Mohammed er-Rahmân at Shubra, to his shop in the Sûk el-Attârin. My eyesight is far from good, Saïd. Do you write as I direct and I will place my name to the letter.'

## II

The words 'well worth your while' had kept time to my steps, or I doubt if I should have survived the odius journey from Shubra. Never can I forget the shape, colour, and especially the weight, of the locked chest which was my burden. Old Mohammed er-Rahmân had accepted my service on the strength of the letter signed by Abdul, and of course, had failed to recognise in 'Saïd' that Hon Neville Kernaby who had had certain confidential dealings with him a year before. But exactly how I was to profit by the fortunate accident which had led Abdul to mistake me for someone called 'Saïd' became more and more obscure as the box grew more and more heavy. So that by the time that I actually arrived with my burden at the entrance to the Street of the Perfumers, my heart had hardened towards Abdul the Know-all; and, setting my box upon the ground, I seated myself upon it to rest and to imprecate at leisure that silent cause of my present exhaustion.

After a time my troubled spirit grew calmer, as I sat there inhaling the insidious breath of Tonquin musk, the fragrance of attár of roses, the sweetness of Indian spikenard and the stinging pungency of myrrh, opoponax, and ihlang-ylang. Faintly I could detect the perfume which I have always counted the most exquisite of all save one – that delightful preparation of Jasmine peculiarly Egyptian. But the mystic breath of frankincense and erotic fumes of ambergris alike left me unmoved; for amid these mingled odours, through which it has always seemed to me that that of cedar runs thematically, I sought in vain for any hint of 'Breath of Allah'.

Fashionable Europe and America were well represented as usual in the Sûk el-Attârin, but the little shop of Mohammed er-Rahmân was quite deserted, although he dealt in the most rare essences of all. Mohammed, however, did not seek Western patronage, nor was there in the heart of the little white-bearded merchant any envy of his seemingly more prosperous neighbours in whose shops New York, London, and Paris smoked amber-scented cigarettes, and whose wares were carried to the uttermost corners of the earth. There is nothing more illusory than the outward seeming of the Eastern merchant. The wealthiest man with whom I was acquainted in the Mûski, had the aspect of a mendicant; and whilst Mohammed's neighbours sold phials of essence and tiny boxes of pastilles to the patrons of Messrs Cook, were not the silent caravans following the ancient desert routes laden with great crates of sweet merchandise from the manufactory at Shubra? To the city of Mecca alone Mohammed sent annually perfumes to the value of two thousand pounds sterling; he manufactured three kinds of incense exclusively for the royal house of Persia; and his wares were known from Alexandria to Kashmîr, and prized alike in Stambûl and Tartary. Well might he watch with tolerant smile the more showy activities of his less fortunate competitors.

The shop of Mohammed er-Rahmân was at the end of the street remote from the Hamzâwi (Cloth Bazaar), and as I stood up to resume my labours my mood of gloomy abstraction was changed as much by a certain atmosphere of expectancy – I cannot otherwise describe it – as by the familiar smells of the place. I had taken no more than three paces onward into the Sûk ere it seemed to me that all business had suddenly become suspended; only the Western element of the throng remained outside whatever influence had claimed the Orientals. Then presently the visitors, also becoming aware of this expectant hush as I had become aware of it, turned almost with one accord, and following the direction of the merchants' glances, gazed up the narrow street towards the Mosque of el-Ashraf.

And here I must chronicle a curious circumstance. Of the Imám Abû Tabâh I had seen nothing for several weeks, but at this moment I suddenly found myself thinking of that remarkable man. Whilst any mention of his name, or nickname – for I could not believe 'Tabâh' to be patronymic – amongst the natives led only to pious ejaculations indicative of respectful fear, by the official world he was tacitly disowned. Yet I had indisputable evidence to show that few doors in Cairo, or indeed in all Egypt, were closed to him; he came and went like a phantom. I should never have been surprised, on entering my private apartments at Shepheard's, to have found him seated therein, nor did I question the veracity of a native acquaintance who assured me that he had met the mysterious *imám* in Aleppo on the same morning that a letter from his partner in Cairo had arrived mentioning a visit by Abû Tabâh to el-Azhar. But throughout the native city he was known as the Magician and was very generally regarded as a master of the *ginn*. Once more depositing my burden upon the ground, then, I gazed with the rest in the direction of the mosque.

It was curious, that moment of perfumed silence, and my imagination, doubtless inspired by the memory of Abû Tabâh, was carried back to the days of the great *khalîfs*, which never seemed far removed from one in those mediaeval streets. I was transported to the Cairo of Harûn al Raschîd, and I thought that the Grand Wazîr on some mission from Baghdad was visiting the Sûk el-Attârin.

Then, stately through the silent group, came a black-robed, white-turbaned figure outwardly similar to many others in the bazaar, but followed by two tall muffled Negroes. So still was the place that I could hear the tap of his ebony stick as he strode along the centre of the street.

At the shop of Mohammed er-Rahmân he paused, exchanging a few words with the merchant, then resumed his way, coming down the Sûk towards me. His glance met mine, as I stood there beside the box; and, to my amazement, he saluted me with smiling dignity and passed on. Had he, too, mistaken me for Saïd? – or had his all-seeing gaze detected beneath my disguise the features of Neville Kernaby?

As he turned out of the narrow street into the Hamzâwi, the commercial uproar was resumed instantly, so that save for this horrible doubt which had set my heart beating with uncomfortable rapidity, by all the evidences now about me his coming might have been a dream.

# III

Filled with misgivings, I carried the box along to the shop; but Mohammed er-Rahmân's greeting held no hint of suspicion.

'By fleetness of foot thou shalt never win Paradise,' he said.

'Nor by unseemly haste shall I thrust others from the path,' I retorted.

'It is idle to bandy words with any acquaintance of Abdul the Porter's,' sighed Mohammed; 'well do I know it. Take up the box and follow me.'

With a key which he carried attached to a chain about his waist, he unlocked the ancient door which alone divided his shop from the outjutting wall marking a bend in the street. A native shop is usually nothing more than a double cell; but descending three stone steps, I found myself in one of those cellar-like apartments which are not uncommon in this part of Cairo. Windows there were none, if I except a small square opening, high up in one of the walls, which evidently communicated with the narrow courtyard separating Mohammed's establishment from that of his neighbour, but which admitted scanty light and less ventilation. Through this opening I could see what looked like the uplifted shafts of a cart. From one of the rough beams of the rather lofty ceiling a brass lamp hung by chains, and a quantity of primitive chemical paraphernalia littered the place; old-fashioned alembics, mysterious-looking jars, and a sort of portable furnace, together with several tripods and a number of large, flat brass pans gave the place the appearance of some old alchemist's den. A rather handsome ebony table, intricately carved and inlaid with mother-o'-pearl and ivory, stood before a cushioned *diwan* which occupied that side of the room in which was the square window.

'Set the box upon the floor,' directed Mohammed, 'but not with such undue dispatch as to cause thyself to sustain any injury.'

That he had been eagerly awaiting the arrival of the box and was now burningly anxious to witness my departure, grew more and more apparent with every word. Therefore –

'There are asses who are fleet of foot,' I said, leisurely depositing my load at his feet; 'but the wise man regulateth his pace in accordance with three things: the heat of the sun; the welfare of others; and the nature of his burden.'

'That thou hast frequently paused on the way from Shubra to reflect upon these three things,' replied Mohammed, 'I cannot doubt; depart, therefore, and ponder them at leisure, for I perceive that thou art a great philosopher.'

'Philosophy,' I continued, seating myself upon the box, 'sustaineth the mind, but the activity of the mind being dependent upon the welfare of the stomach, even the philosopher cannot afford to labour without hire.'

At that, Mohammed er-Rahmân unloosed upon me a long pent-up torrent of invective – and furnished me with the information which I was seeking.

'O son of a wall-eyed mule!' he cried, shaking his fists over me, 'no longer will I suffer thy idiotic chatter! Return to Abdul the Porter, who employed thee, for not one *faddah* will I give thee, calamitous mongrel that thou art! Depart! For I was but this moment informed that a lady of high station is about to visit me. Depart! Lest she mistake my shop for a pigsty!'

But even as he spoke the words, I became aware of a vague disturbance in the street, and –

'Ah!' cried Mohammed, running to the foot of the steps and gazing upwards, 'now am I utterly undone! Shame of thy parents that thou art, it is now unavoidable that the Lady Zuleyka shall find thee in my shop. Listen, offensive insect – thou art Said my assistant. Utter not one word; or with this' – to my great alarm he produced a dangerous-looking pistol from beneath his robe – 'will I blow a hole through thy vacuous skull!'

Hastily concealing the pistol, he went hurrying up the steps, in time to perform a low salutation before a veiled woman who was accompanied by a Sûdanese servant-girl and a Negro. Exchanging some words with her which I was unable to detect, Mohammed er-Rahmân led the way down into the apartment wherein I stood, followed by the lady, who in turn was followed by her servant. The Negro remained above. Perceiving me as she entered, the lady, who was attired with extraordinary elegance, paused, glancing at Mohammed.

'My lady,' he began immediately, bowing before her, 'it is Saïd, my assistant, the slothfulness of whose habits is only exceeded by the impudence of his conversation.'

She hesitated, bestowing upon me a glance of her beautiful eyes. Despite the gloom of the place and the *yashmak* which she wore, it was manifest that she was good to look upon. A faint but exquisite perfume stole to my nostrils, whereby I knew that Mohammed's charming visitor was none other than the Lady Zuleyka.

'Yet,' she said softly, 'he hath the look of an active young man.'

'His activity,' replied the scent merchant, 'resideth entirely in his tongue.'

The Lady Zuleyka seated herself upon the *dîwan*, looking all about the apartment.

'Everything is in readiness, Mohammed?' she asked.

'Everything, my lady.'

Again the beautiful eyes were turned in my direction, and, as their inscrutable gaze rested upon me, a scheme –

which, since it was never carried out, need not be described – presented itself to my mind. Following a brief but eloquent silence – for my answering glances were laden with significance:

'O Mohammed,' said the Lady Zuleyka indolently, 'in what manner doth a merchant, such as thyself, chastise his servants when their conduct displeaseth him?'

Mohammed er-Rahmân seemed somewhat at a loss for a reply, and stood there staring foolishly.

'I have whips for mine,' murmured the soft voice. 'It is an old custom of my family.'

Slowly she cast her eyes in my direction once more.

'It seemed to me, O Saïd,' she continued, gracefully resting one jewelled hand upon the ebony table, 'that thou hadst presumed to cast love-glances upon me. There is one waiting above whose duty it is to protect me from such insults. Miska!' – to the servant girl – 'summon El-Kimri [The Dove].'

Whilst I stood there dumbfounded and abashed the girl called up the steps:

'El-Kimri! Come hither!'

Instantly there burst into the room the form of that hideous Negro whom I had glimpsed above; and –

'O Kimri,' directed the Lady Zuleyka, and languidly extended her hand in my direction, 'throw this presumptuous clown into the street!'

*A magazine illustration conveying the interest in Egyptology in the early years of this century – an interest that was widespread.*

*A hooded magician and disciples dabble in the black arts.*

My discomfiture had proceeded far enough, and I recognised that, at whatever risk of discovery, I must act instantly. Therefore, at the moment that El-Kimri reached the foot of the steps, I dashed my left fist into his grinning face, putting all my weight behind the blow, which I followed up with a short right, utterly outraging the pugilistic proprieties, since it was well below the belt. El-Kimri bit the dust to the accompaniment of a human discord composed of three notes – and I leapt up the steps, turned to the left, and ran off around the Mosque of el-Ashraf, where I speedily lost myself in the crowded Ghurîya.

Beneath their factitious duskiness my cheeks were burning hotly: I was ashamed of my execrable artistry. For a druggist's assistant does not lightly make love to a duchess!

# IV

I spent the remainder of the forenoon at my house in the Darb el-Ahmar heaping curses upon my own fatuity and upon the venerable head of Abdul the Know-all. At one moment it seemed to me that I had wantonly destroyed a golden opportunity, at the next that the seeming opportunity had been a mere mirage. With the passing of noon and the approach of evening I sought desperately for a plan, knowing that if I failed to conceive one by midnight, another chance of seeing the famous prescription would probably not present itself for twelve months.

At about four o'clock in the afternoon came the dawn of a hazy idea, and since it necessitated a visit to my rooms at Shepheard's, I washed the paint off my face and hands, changed, hurried to the hotel, ate a hasty meal, and returned to the Darb el-Ahmar, where I resumed my disguise.

There are some who have criticised me harshly in regard to my commercial activities at this time, and none of my affairs has provoked greater acerbitude than that of the perfume called 'Breath of Allah'. Yet I am at a loss to perceive wherein my perfidy lay; for my outlook is sufficiently socialistic to cause me to regard with displeasure the conserving by an individual of something which, without loss to himself, might reasonably be shared by the community. For this reason I have always resented the way in which the Moslem veils the faces of the pearls of his *harêm*. And whilst the success of my present enterprise would not render the Lady Zuleyka the poorer, it would enrich and beautify the world by delighting the senses of men with a perfume more exquisite than any hitherto known.

Such were my reflections as I made my way through the dark and deserted bazaar quarter, following the Shâria el-Akkadi to the Mosque of el-Ashraf. There I turned to the left in the direction of the Hamzâwi, until, coming to the narrow alley opening from it into the Sûk el-Attârin, I plunged into its darkness, which was like that of a tunnel, although the upper parts of the houses above were silvered by the moon.

I was making for that cramped little courtyard adjoining the shop of Mohammed er-Rahmân in which I had observed the presence of one of those narrow high-wheeled carts peculiar to the district, and as the entrance thereto from the Sûk was closed by a rough wooden fence I anticipated little difficulty in gaining access. Yet there was one difficulty which I had not foreseen, and which I had not met with had I arrived, as I might easily have arranged to do, a little earlier. Coming to the corner of the Street of the Perfumers, I cautiously protruded my head in order to survey the prospect.

Abû Tabâh was standing immediately outside the shop of Mohammed er-Rahmân!

My heart gave a great leap as I drew back into the shadow,

for I counted his presence of evil omen to the success of my enterprise. Then, a swift revelation, the truth burst in upon my mind. He was there in the capacity of *imâm* and attendant magician at the mystical 'Blessing of the perfumes'! With cautious tread I retraced my steps, circled round the Mosque and made for the narrow street which runs parallel with that of the Perfumers and into which I knew the courtyard beside Mohammed's shop must open. What I did not know was how I was going to enter it from that end.

I experienced unexpected difficulty in locating the place, for the height of the buildings about me rendered it impossible to pick up any familiar landmark. Finally, having twice retraced my steps, I determined that a door of old but strong workmanship set in a high, thick wall must communicate with the courtyard; for I could see no other opening to the right or left through which it would have been possible for a vehicle to pass.

Mechanically I tried the door, but, as I had anticipated, found it to be securely locked. A profound silence reigned all about me and there was no window in sight from which my operations could be observed. Therefore, having planned out my route, I determined to scale the wall. My first foothold was offered by the heavy wooden lock which projected fully six inches from the door. Above it was a crossbeam and then a gap of several inches between the top of the gate and the arch into which it was built. Above the arch projected an iron rod from which depended a hook; and if I could reach the bar it would be possible to get astride the wall.

I reached the bar successfully, and although it proved to be none too firmly fastened, I took the chance and without making very much noise found myself perched aloft and looking down into the little court. A sigh of relief escaped me; for the narrow cart with its disproportionate wheels stood there as I had seen it in the morning, its shafts pointing gauntly upward to where the moon of the prophet's nativity swam in a cloudless sky. A dim light shone out from the square window of Mohammed er-Rahmân's cellar.

Having studied the situation very carefully, I presently perceived to my great satisfaction that whilst the tail of the cart was wedged under a crossbar, which retained it in its position, one of the shafts was in reach of my hand. Thereupon I entrusted my weight to the shaft, swinging out over the well of the courtyard. So successful was I that only a faint creaking sound resulted; and I descended into the vehicle almost silently.

Having assured myself that my presence was undiscovered by Abû Tabâh, I stood up cautiously, my hands resting upon the wall, and peered through the little window into the room. Its appearance had changed somewhat. The lamp was lighted and shed a weird and subdued illumination upon a rough table placed almost beneath it. Upon this table were scales, measures, curiously shaped flasks, and odd-looking chemical apparatus which might have been made in the days of Avicenna himself. At one end of the table stood an alembic over a little pan in which burnt a spirituous flame. Mohammed er-Rahmân was placing cushions upon the *diwan* immediately beneath me, but there was no one else in the room. Glancing upward, I noted that the height of the neighbouring building prevented the moonlight from penetrating into the courtyard, so that my presence could not be detected by means of any light from without; and, since the whole of the upper part of the room was shadowed, I saw little cause for apprehension within.

At this moment came the sound of a car approaching along the Sharia esh-Sharawani. I heard it stop, near the Mosque of el-Ashraf, and in the almost perfect stillness of those tortuous streets from which by day arises a very babel of tongues I heard approaching footsteps. I crouched down in the cart, as the footsteps came nearer, passed the end of the courtyard abutting on the Street of the Perfumers, and paused before the shop of Mohammed er-Rahmân. The musical voice of Abû Tabâh spoke and that of the Lady Zuleka answered. Came a loud rapping, and the creak of an opening door: then –

'Descend the steps, place the coffer on the table, and

then remain immediately outside the door,' continued the imperious voice of the lady. 'Make sure that there are no eavesdroppers.'

Faintly through the little window there reached my ears a sound as of some heavy object being placed upon a wooden surface, then a muffled disturbance as of several persons entering the room; finally, the muffled bang of a door closed and barred . . . and soft footsteps in the adjoining street!

Crouching down in the cart and almost holding my breath, I watched through a hole in the side of the ramshackle vehicle that fence to which I have already referred as closing the end of the courtyard which adjoined the Sûk el-Attârin. A spear of moonlight, penetrating through some gap in the surrounding buildings, silvered its extreme edge. To an accompaniment of much kicking and heavy breathing, into this natural limelight arose the black countenance of 'The Dove'. To my unbounded joy I perceived that his nose was lavishly decorated with sticking-plaster and that his right eye was temporarily off duty. Eight fat fingers clutching at the top of the woodwork, the bloated Negro regarded the apparently empty yard for a space of some three seconds, ere lowering his ungainly bulk to the level of the street again. Followed a faint 'pop' and a gurgling quite unmistakable. I heard him walking back to the door, as I cautiously stood up and again surveyed the interior of the room.

# V

Egypt, as the earliest historical records show, has always been a land of magic, and according to native belief it is today the theatre of many supernatural dramas. For my own part, prior to the episode which I am about to relate, my personal experiences of the kind had been limited and unconvincing. That Abû Tabâh possessed a sort of uncanny power akin to second sight, I knew, but I regarded it merely as a form of telepathy. His presence at the preparation of the secret perfume did not surprise me, for a belief in the efficacy of magical operations prevailed, as I was aware, even among the more cultured Moslems. My scepticism, however, was about to be rudely shaken.

As I raised my head above the ledge of the window and looked into the room, I perceived the Lady Zuleyka seated on the cushioned *dîwan*, her hands resting upon an open roll of parchment which lay upon the table beside a massive brass chest of antique native workmanship. The lid of the chest was raised, and the interior seemed to be empty, but near it upon the table I observed a number of gold-stoppered vessels of Venetian glass and each of which was of a different colour.

Beside a brazier wherein glowed a charcoal fire, Abû Tabâh stood; and into the fire he cast alternately strips of paper bearing writing of some sort and little dark brown pastilles which he took from a sandalwood box set upon a sort of tripod beside him. They were composed of some kind of aromatic gum in which benzoin seemed to predominate, and the fumes from the brazier filled the room with a blue mist.

The *imám*, in his soft, musical voice, was reciting that chapter of the Korân called 'The Angel'. The weird ceremony had begun. In order to achieve my purpose I perceived that I should have to draw myself right up to the narrow embrasure and rest my weight entirely upon the ledge of the window. There was little danger in the manoeuvre, provided I made no noise; for the hanging lamp, by reason of its form, cast no light into the upper part of the room. As I achieved the desired position I became painfully aware of the pungency of the perfume with which the apartment was filled.

Lying there upon the ledge in a most painful attitude, I wriggled forward inch by inch further into the room, until I was in a position to use my right arm more or less freely. The preliminary prayer concluded, the measuring of the perfumes had now actually commenced, and I readily perceived that without recourse to the parchment, from which the Lady Zuleyka never once removed her hands, it would indeed be impossible to discover the secret. For, consulting the ancient prescription, she would select one of the gold-stoppered bottles, unscrew it, direct that so many grains should be taken from it, and never removing her gaze from Mohammed er-Rahmân whilst he measured out the correct quantity, would restopper the vessel and so proceed. As each was placed in a wide-mouthed glass jar by the perfumer, Abû Tabâh, extending his hands over the jar, pronounced the names:

'Gabraîl, Mikaîl, Israfîl, Israîl.'

Cautiously I raised to my eyes the small but powerful opera-glasses to procure which I had gone to my rooms at Shepheard's. Focusing them upon the ancient scroll lying on the table beneath me, I discovered, to my joy, that I could read the lettering quite well. Whilst Abû Tabâh began to recite some kind of incantation in the course of which the names of the Companions of the Prophet frequently occurred, I commenced to read the writing of Avicenna.

'In the name of God, the Compassionate, the Merciful, the High, the Great. . . .'

So far had I proceeded and no further when I became aware of a curious change in the form of the Arabic letters. They seemed to be moving, to be cunningly changing places one with another as if to trick me out of grasping their meaning!

The illusion persisting, I determined that it was due to the unnatural strain imposed upon my vision, and although I recognised that time was precious I found myself compelled temporarily to desist, since nothing was to be gained by watching these letters which danced from side to side of the parchment, sometimes in groups and sometimes singly, so that I found myself pursuing one slim Arab A ('*Alif*) entirely up the page from the bottom to the top where it finally disappeared under the thumb of the Lady Zuleyka!

Lowering the glasses I stared down in stupefaction at Abû Tabâh. He had just cast fresh incense upon the flames, and it came home to me, with a childish and unreasoning sense of terror, that the Egyptians who called this man the Magician were wiser than I. For whilst I could no longer hear his voice, I now could *see* the words issuing from his mouth! They formed slowly and gracefully in the blue clouds of vapour some four feet above his head, revealed their meaning to me in letters of gold, and then faded away towards the ceiling!

Old-established beliefs began to totter about me as I became aware of a number of small murmuring voices within the room. They were the voices of the perfumes burning in the brazier. Said one, in a guttural tone:

'I am Myrrh. My voice is the voice of the Tomb.'

And another softly: 'I am Ambergris. I lure the hearts of men.'

And a third huskily: 'I am Patchouli. My promises are lies.'

My sense of smell seemed to have deserted me and to

have been replaced by a sense of hearing. And now this room of magic began to expand before my eyes. The walls receded and receded, until the apartment grew larger than the interior of the Citadel Mosque; the roof shot up so high that I knew there was no cathedral in the world half so lofty. Abû Tabâh, his hands extended above the brazier, shrank to minute dimensions, and the Lady Zuleyka, seated beneath me, became almost invisible.

The project which had led me to thrust myself into the midst of this feast of sorcery vanished from my mind. I desired but one thing: to depart, ere reason utterly deserted me. But, to my horror, I discovered that my muscles had become rigid bands of iron! The figure of Abû Tabâh was drawing nearer; his slowly moving arms had grown serpentine and his eyes had changed to pools of flame which seemed to summon me. At the time when this new phenomenon added itself to the other horrors, I seemed to be impelled by an irresistible force to jerk my head downwards: I heard my neck muscles snap metallically: I *saw* a scream of agony spurt forth from my lips . . . and I saw upon a little ledge immediately below the square window a little *mibkharah*, or incense burner, which hitherto I had not observed. A thick, oily brown stream of vapour was issuing from its perforated lid and bathing my face clammily. Sense of smell I had none; but a chuckling, demoniacal voice spoke from the *mibkharah*, saying –

33

'I am *Hashish*! I drive men mad! Whilst thou hast lain up there like a very fool, I have sent my vapours to thy brain and stolen thy senses from thee. It was for this purpose that I was set here beneath the window where thou couldst not fail to enjoy the full benefit of my poisonous perfume. . . .'

Slipping off the ledge, I fell . . . and darkness closed about me.

# VI

My awakening constitutes one of the most painful recollections of a not uneventful career; for, with aching head and tortured limbs, I sat upright upon the floor of a tiny, stuffy, and unclean cell! The only light was that which entered by way of a little grating in the door. I was a prisoner; and, in the same instant that I realised the fact of my incarceration, I realised also that I had been duped. The weird happenings in the apartment of Mohammed er-Rahmân had been hallucinations due to my having inhaled the fumes of some preparation of *hashish*, or Indian hemp. The characteristic sickly odour of the drug had been concealed by the pungency of the other and more odoriferous perfumes; and because of the position of the censer containing the burning *hashish*, no one else in the room had been affected by its vapour. Could it have been that Abû Tabâh had known of my presence from the first?

I rose, unsteadily, and looked out through the grating into a narrow passage. A native constable stood at one end of it, and beyond him I obtained a glimpse of the entrance hall. Instantly I recognised that I was under arrest at the Bâb el-Khalk police station!

A great rage consumed me. Raising my fists I banged furiously upon the door, and the Egyptian policeman came running along the passage.

'What does this mean, *shawêsh?*' I demanded. 'Why am I detained here? I am an Englishman. Send the superintendent to me instantly.'

The policeman's face expressed alternately anger, surprise, and stupefaction.

You were brought here last night, most disgustingly and speechlessly drunk, in a cart!' he replied.

'I demand to see the superintendent.'

'Certainly, certainly, *effendim!*' cried the man, now thoroughly alarmed. 'In an instant, *effendim!*'

Such is the magical power of the word 'Inglisi' (Englishman).

A painfully perturbed and apologetic native official appeared almost immediately, to whom I explained that I had been to a fancy dress ball at the Gezira Palace Hotel, and, injudiciously walking homeward at a late hour, had been attacked and struck senseless. He was anxiously courteous, sending a man to Shepheard's with my written instructions to bring back a change of apparel and offering me every facility for removing my disguise and making myself presentable. The fact that he palpably disbelieved my story did not render his concern one whit the less.

I discovered the hour to be close upon noon, and, once more my outward self, I was about to depart from the Place Bâb el-Khalk, when, into the superintendent's room came

Abû Tabâh! His handsome ascetic face exhibited grave concern as he saluted me.

'How can I express my sorrow, Kernaby Pasha,' he said in his soft faultless English, 'that so unfortunate and unseemly an accident should have befallen you? I learned of your presence here but a few moments ago, and I hastened to convey to you an assurance of my deepest regret and sympathy.'

'More than good of you,' I replied. 'I am much indebted.'

'It grieves me,' he continued suavely, 'to learn that there are footpads infesting the Cairo streets, and that an English gentleman may not walk home from a ball safely. I trust that you will provide the police with a detailed account of any valuables which you may have lost. I have here' – thrusting his hand into his robes – 'the only item of your property thus far recovered. No doubt you are somewhat short-sighted, Kernaby Pasha, as I am, and experience a certain difficulty in discerning the names of your partners upon your dance programme.'

And with one of those sweet smiles which could so transfigure his face, Abû Tabâh handed me my opera-glasses!

www.ingramcontent.com/pod-product-compliance
Lightning Source LLC
Chambersburg PA
CBHW030531260626
47157CB00005B/1977